Jack and the Beanstalk

My First Reading Book

Story retold by Janet Brown
Illustrations by Ken Morton

ARMADILLO

A poor widow lived with her only son, Jack, in a small cottage. They had no money and the widow struggled to feed them.

Every day she told her son, "You must find a job!"

And every day Jack replied, "I'll find a job tomorrow."

Why did the poor widow want Jack to find a job?

Times were hard, and soon the widow had to sell her old brown cow. "You must take her to market," she told Jack. "Make sure you get a good price!"

On the way, Jack met the butcher. "If you give me your fine cow, I will pay you with these magic beans," said the butcher.

So Jack sold the cow and brought home the beans.

His mother was furious. "You silly boy!" she cried. "Now what will we eat?" And she threw the beans out of the window.

What did Jack accept in return for his mother's old brown cow?

The next morning there was a giant beanstalk in the garden, exactly where the beans had landed!

"It must be magic!" thought Jack, and he began to climb the beanstalk. He climbed for miles into the sky and finally he saw a huge castle floating on a cloud.

The castle belonged to a wicked ogre who ate people for fun. Jack tiptoed inside and when he heard the ogre returning, he crept into the oven to hide.

What did Jack find at the top of the beanstalk, and who did it belong to?

The ogre came into the kitchen roaring this song:

"Fee fi fo fum
I smell the blood of an Englishman!
Be he alive or be he dead
I'll grind his bones to make my bread!"

Then, seeing no one around, he set a large white goose upon the table. "Lay!" he commanded, and the goose laid a golden egg. "Lay!" he said again, and the goose laid another golden egg.

When there were twelve eggs on the table, the ogre fell asleep.

What was special about the ogre's large white goose?

Jack climbed quietly out of the oven. He tucked the goose under his arm and he ran out of the castle and down the beanstalk as fast as his legs would carry him.

At home, he showed the goose to his mother. "Lay!" commanded Jack, and the goose laid a golden egg.

Jack's mother was so happy, she burst into tears. Soon they had all the food they needed.

*What did Jack steal
from the ogre's castle?*

But Jack was longing for another adventure, so back he climbed, up the beanstalk. When the ogre returned to his castle, Jack was hiding in the cupboard. Again, the ogre roared:

"Fee fi fo fum
I smell the blood of an Englishman!
Be he alive or be he dead
I'll grind his bones to make my bread!"

Then, seeing no one around, he sat down and counted his money. Soon he fell asleep.

Jack climbed quietly out of the cupboard. He tucked the money-bags under his arm and he ran out of the castle and down the beanstalk as fast as his legs would carry him.

At home, he showed the money to his delighted mother.

Where did Jack hide from the ogre this time?

Soon Jack was longing for *another* adventure, so back he climbed, up the beanstalk. When the ogre returned to his castle, Jack was hiding in the wooden chest. Again, the ogre roared:

"Fee fi fo fum
I smell the blood of an Englishman!
Be he alive or be he dead
I'll grind his bones to make my bread!"

Then, seeing no one around, he set a golden harp upon the table. "Play!" he commanded and the harp played beautiful music. "Stop!" commanded the ogre at last, and he fell asleep.

Why did Jack climb up the beanstalk a third time?

Jack climbed quietly out of the cupboard. He tucked the harp under his arm, and then he ran as fast as his legs would carry him.

But the harp cried out, "Master! Master!" and the ogre woke up!

What happened when Jack tried to run away with the ogre's magic harp?

The ogre chased Jack out of the castle and down the beanstalk.

"Quick, Mother, bring the hatchet!" cried Jack, and he chopped the beanstalk down.

So that was the end of the ogre. And Jack and his mother were rich and happy for the rest of their lives.

How did Jack manage to escape from the ogre?

On a piece of paper, try writing these words.
Can you find them again in the story?

beans

old brown cow

goose

hatchet

golden eggs